■ AN EDWARD THE UNREADY BOOK ■

EDWARD'S
OVERWHELMING OVERNIGHT

· ROSEMARY WELLS ·

Dial Books for Young Readers *New York*

for Atha

The telephone rang. It interrupted Edward's story.
"I'm sure he'd love to come," said Edward's mother.

"Won't it be fun to play in the snow
at Anthony's house!" said Edward's father.

"Will you come back for me soon?" asked Edward.
"Of course!" answered his mother and father.

Anthony's mother welcomed everyone
into the kitchen.

"Promise you will come back soon?" asked Edward.
"We promise!" answered his mother and father.

Edward and Anthony made a snowman.
Snow began to fall.

Soon it was snowing so hard, they could not see.
"Cocoa time!" called Anthony's mother.

The telephone rang. It was Edward's mother.
"The snow is too deep to drive the car safely," she said.

"You'll have to spend the night at Anthony's house.
Be brave, my little cupcake!"

"Would you like to play with my train?" asked Anthony.
"No," said Edward.

"Would you like a fudge roll?" asked Anthony.
"No, thank you," said Edward.

Edward would not eat supper.
His mother and father called to say good night.

"Now you feel better!" said Anthony's mother.
But Edward did not feel better.

Even in Anthony's new pajamas Edward
would not sleep.

Anthony's mother and father couldn't stand it.

So Anthony's mother dug a path to the car.

Anthony's father put chains on the tires.

They followed the snowplow all the way
to Edward's house.

"I was not ready for overnights away from home," said Anthony's father, "until I was twenty-one years old!"

"He wasn't quite ready," explained Anthony's father.
"He *is* ready for cinnamon toast," said Edward's mother.

"And I'll bet you're ready for a bedtime story,"
said Edward's father.

During Edward's story the telephone rang.
But no one answered it.

This edition printed for Troll Communications, L.L.C.

Published by Dial Books for Young Readers
A Division of Penguin Books USA Inc.
375 Hudson Street
New York, New York 10014

Library of Congress Cataloging in Publication Data
Wells, Rosemary.
Edward's overwhelming overnight / Rosemary Wells.
p.   cm.—(Edward the unready)
Summary: Edward's parents tell him that because
of the snow he will have to stay overnight with
his friend Anthony, but Edward finds this overwhelming.
ISBN 0-8037-1883-7
[1. Bears—Fiction. 2. Sleepovers—Fiction.
3. Snow—Fiction. 4. Growth—Fiction.]
I. Title. II. Series: Wells, Rosemary. Edward the unready.
PZ7.W46843Ed 1995 [E]—dc20 95-4281 CIP AC

*The artwork for each picture
is an ink drawing with watercolor painting.*